When Hugo Went to School

by Anne Rockwell

Macmillan Publishing Company   New York

Collier Macmillan Canada   Toronto

Maxwell Macmillan International Publishing Group
New York   Oxford   Singapore   Sydney

for Julianna Joy

Printed and bound in Singapore   First Edition

10 9 8 7 6 5 4 3 2 1

The text of this book is set in 20 point ITC Newtext Book.
The illustrations are rendered in pen and ink and water-
color on paper.

Library of Congress Cataloging-in-Publication Data
Rockwell, Anne F.
  When Hugo went to school / by Anne Rockwell. — 1st ed.
    p.   cm.
  Summary: Following his new friends to school lands
Hugo the dog in jail.
  ISBN 0-02-777305-1
  [1. Dogs—Fiction. 2. Schools—Fiction.] I. Title.
PZ7.R5943Ht 1990 [E]—dc20   89-13211

Hugo's friend went to visit
his sister and her family.
Hugo went, too.

The sister and her husband had three children
named Maggie, Matthew, and Jake.
Hugo liked them very much.

He wanted to play with them all day long.

So, in the morning,
when Maggie, Matthew, and Jake
went out the gate,

and down the street

around the corner,
on their way to school,
Hugo followed them.

The principal of the school said,
"Good morning!" with a smile
  to all the children.
  But when she saw Hugo she said,
"Go home!"
  She would not let Hugo come in.
"Be a good boy
  and go home now, Hugo,"
  said Maggie.

But Hugo had forgotten the way back
to his friend's sister's house.
Besides, he wanted to go to school
with the children because
it looked like so much fun.
So he sat down
and waited politely
for the principal to let him come in.

After a while

Hugo got tired of waiting quietly

outside the school.

He began to ask to come in,

quite loudly.

So the principal asked a policeman

to come and get Hugo.

A policeman came and said to Hugo,
"Come on, big boy!"
He gave Hugo a dog biscuit,
put a leash on Hugo
and scratched him behind the ears.
Then Hugo rode away
in the policeman's car.

When the policeman got to
the police station he said,
"Look at this nice big boy
who wanted to go to school."
Then the policeman put Hugo in a cage.
Hugo didn't like that.
The he called the telephone number
on the little tag on Hugo's collar.
That was Hugo's friend's telephone number
in their own apartment far away.

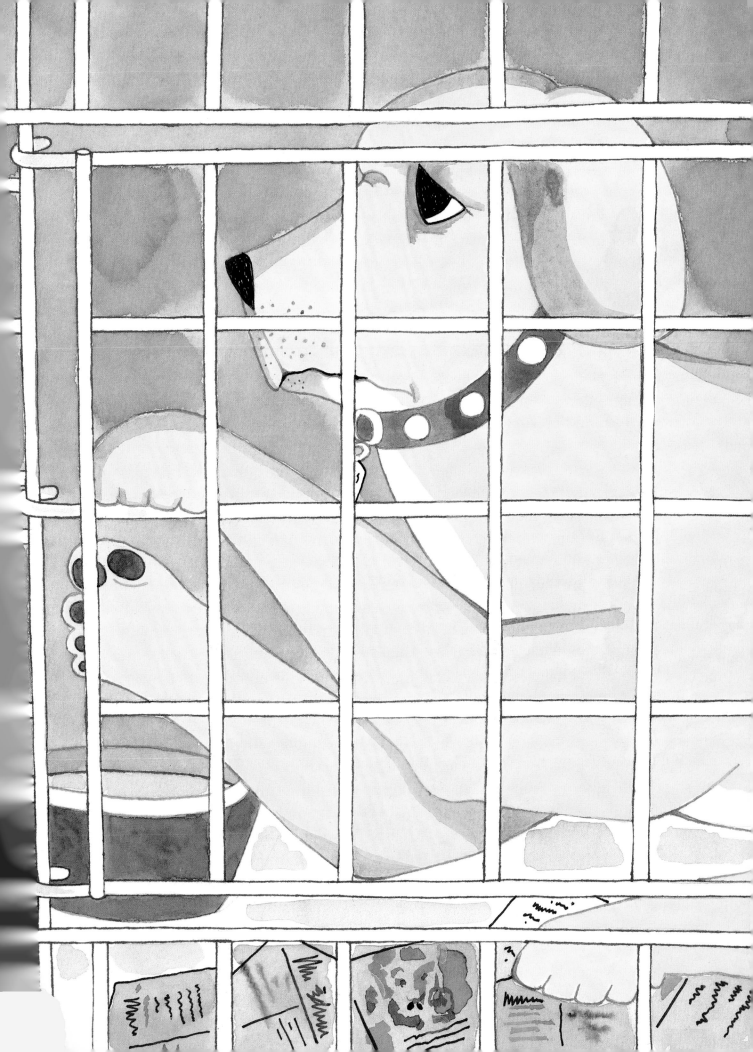

But no one answered the telephone.
That was because Hugo's friend
was at his sister's house
in another town.
The apartment was empty
and the telephone rang and rang.
And while the telephone
was ringing and ringing
in their empty apartment

Hugo's friend was going up and down
his sister's street calling,
"Come, Hugo! Hugo, come!"

But Hugo could not come
to his friend.
He could not even hear
his friend calling him
from up and down
his sister's street.

Hugo's friend was very sad because
Hugo had not come when he called him.
But suddenly his sister said,

"I will call the police station
and ask if they have seen Hugo.
Cheer up until we hear what they say."

Hugo's friend was very, very happy
when he came to get Hugo
at the police station.
Hugo was extremely glad to see him, too.

The next day Hugo and his friend
said good-bye and drove away.
It was almost dark
when they got home again.
"It is nice to go visiting,"
said Hugo's friend,
"but I am always glad to be home again."

Hugo wagged his tail.

That was how he said, "Me, too!"